9/09

D1412362

TENNIS
LIAR

BY JAKE MADDOX

illustrated by Sean Tiffany

text by Chris Kreie

J
mAD

Impact Books are published by Stone Arch Books
151 Good Counsel Drive, P.O. Box 669
Mankato, Minnesota 56002
www.stonearchbooks.com

Library of Congress Cataloging-in-Publication Data
Maddox, Jake.
    Tennis liar / by Jake Maddox; text by Chris Kreie;
illustrated by Sean Tiffany.
        p. cm. — (Impact books. A Jake Maddox sports story)
        ISBN 978-1-4342-1597-0
        [1. Tennis—Fiction.] I. Kreie, Chris. II. Tiffany, Sean, ill. III. Title.
PZ7.M25643Tdp 2010
[Fic]—dc22   2009004096

Summary:
When his friend Max asks him to join a tennis league, Henry can't say
no. It's expensive, so Max's dad pays Henry's way. Henry can't tell his
dad, or he'll have to give up tennis for good. Is being able to play the
game he loves worth hiding the truth?

Creative Director: Heather Kindseth
Graphic Designer: Carla Zetina-Yglesias

TABLE OF CONTENTS

CHAPTER 1

CHAMPIONSHIP MATCH

Henry looked across the net and waited for the serve. His opponent struck the ball.

Quickly, Henry moved to his right and swung his racquet back. He stepped toward the ball and ripped a wicked shot across the net. The ball soared deep into the corner.

His opponent reached his racquet for the ball, but he couldn't get it. Henry had scored another point.

Henry had already won the first set of the match. In the second set, he was ahead five games to two. The first player to win two sets would win the match. If Henry could win this set, he'd be the match winner. He knew he could do it.

Henry loved tennis. Even though this was his first summer playing, he thought it was way more fun than any other sport he had ever played.

Max, Henry's best friend, had convinced him to play. Now tennis was taking over Henry's life. He played for hours nearly every day.

Thanks to all the practice, Henry had gotten really good. Now he was playing for the third-place trophy in the final city tournament of the summer.

"Get him, Henry," yelled Max from behind the fence. "Finish him off!"

Henry heard Max's voice, but he didn't turn to look at his friend. Instead, he stayed focused on the match.

His opponent launched another serve. The ball again came toward Henry's right-hand side, his forehand side. Henry's forehand was his strongest side. Hitting from his left side, his backhand side, was a lot harder. Henry knew his backhand needed more practice.

Henry cocked his racquet behind his body. Then he took a big swing. The ball flew over the net, and his opponent hit a soft shot back. The ball landed short on Henry's side of the court, so he ran up to hit it. After striking the ball, he moved toward the net.

The other player barely got to the ball. He sent a floater toward Henry at the net. Henry waited for the ball to come down. At just the right moment, he swung his racquet over his head. Finally, he smashed the ball hard into his opponent's court.

The other player didn't stand a chance. The ball landed, bounced, and crashed loudly into the back fence.

Henry had won! He had won the match and the third-place trophy.

CHAPTER 2

FREE FEES

After the tournament, Henry and Max rode their bikes home. Both boys had their tennis bags slung over their backs.

"You played so great today," said Max. "Your first summer of tennis, and you took third place. That's amazing!"

"It was pretty awesome," said Henry.

"So are you going to play in the fall indoor league with me?" asked Max.

"I don't know," said Henry. "I'd like to, but . . ."

"But what?" Max asked. "You have to play. It's the Oak Point Breakers. We're the best team in the city."

"I know. I'd love to play," Henry said.

"So what's the problem?" asked Max.

"I don't know," said Henry. "How much does the league cost, anyway?"

"I think it's seven hundred dollars," said Max.

"Seven hundred dollars?!" said Henry. "Then there's your answer. No way is my dad going to pay seven hundred bucks for me to play tennis."

"I bet my dad would pay for your fees," said Max.

"Why would he do that?" asked Henry.

"Why not?" asked Max. "He's got the money. Besides, he's the team coach and a big shot at the tennis club."

"My dad would never go for that," said Henry. "Seven hundred dollars is too much. He wouldn't want to spend that much money on tennis."

"Then don't tell him," said Max. "Don't tell him my dad is paying."

"I can't lie to my dad," Henry said quietly.

"It wouldn't be a lie," said Max. "You just wouldn't be telling him the whole truth."

"That's not much of a difference," said Henry.

They reached the dirt road that led to Henry's house. Henry slowed down.

"Well, it's up to you," said Max. "All I know is that you need to play. And you shouldn't let your dad stop you."

"Easy for you to say," said Henry.

"I'll talk to you later," said Max, pedaling ahead. "Just remember, we need you on our team, man. We need you."

"I'll think about it," Henry called after him. He turned and pedaled toward his house.

CHAPTER 3

FALL LEAGUE OR FOOTBALL?

Henry dropped his bike on the grass next to his house and burst through the back door. His parents were sitting at the kitchen table, reading the newspaper.

"Hey, Mom and Dad," said Henry. "Look!" He held up the trophy he had won at the tournament.

"Third place?" Mom said. "That's really terrific, honey." She stood up and gave Henry a hug.

"Want to see, Dad?" asked Henry.

"Of course," said his father. Max's dad had his face buried in the newspaper.

Henry walked over to him. "It's third place," he said. "Not as good as first or second, but since this was my first season, I'm really happy."

Henry's dad barely looked away from his paper for two seconds. "Good job, son," he said.

Henry frowned and looked at his mom. She gave him a little smile. "You did great, honey," Mom said.

"So, Henry," said his dad. "I'm reading about the Bears training camp. That new quarterback seems to be pretty talented. I can't wait for football season to start. How about you?"

"Actually, I wanted to talk to you about that," Henry said.

Dad looked up. "Yeah?" he asked. "What is it?"

"I don't want to play football this season," Henry said.

Henry's dad put his paper down. "What? Why?" he asked.

"I want to play tennis, in an indoor league with Max," Henry explained.

"You want to quit the team?" Dad asked.

"I want to play tennis, Dad," said Henry.

"Honey, you've seen this coming for a long time," Mom told Dad. "Henry has never loved football like you do."

Henry's father let out a big sigh. He folded up his newspaper.

"Yeah, I know," he said. Then he turned to Henry and said, "You really love it, don't you?"

"Yeah, I do," said Henry.

"Well, then," said his father, "I think you need to play tennis."

"Are you serious?" asked Henry.

"Of course I am," said his father. "You go join that team and you give it everything you have, okay?"

"I will," said Henry, grinning. "Thanks!"

Henry was thrilled. He got to play in the league, and since Dad hadn't asked about the fees, Henry hadn't had to lie. He couldn't wait to tell Max the great news.

CHAPTER 4

THE CLUB

Henry pulled open the large double glass doors of the Oak Point City Tennis Club and walked inside.

A pretty girl behind a desk asked, "May I help you?"

"I'm here to see Max Martinson," Henry said.

"I'll have him paged right away, sir," said the receptionist.

Henry had never been called "sir" before. He felt out of place in the large, fancy lobby.

Water trickled down a marble fountain in the corner. Soft piano music filled the air. He thought he should sit down, but the chairs looked too nice to sit on.

"May I get you something to drink?" asked the girl. "An energy drink, an iced coffee, a bottle of water?"

"No thank you," said Henry.

"Hey, buddy!" said Max as he crashed through a door next to the desk. "First day of the indoor season. This is going to be awesome."

Henry smiled at the receptionist. Then Max led him through the door and into the club.

"Let's go to the locker room," said Max.

As the two of them walked through the club, Henry noticed coolers loaded with sports drinks and tables piled high with energy bars. "Are those free?" asked Henry.

"Of course," said Max, laughing. "Have one." He tossed an energy bar to Henry.

They rounded a corner and stepped into an open room. Big leather chairs sat in the middle of the room. Flat-screen TVs hung from one wall. Along the other walls were tall, open lockers.

"This is the locker room?" asked Henry.

"Yes. You like it?" asked Max.

"It's unbelievable," said Henry.

"Come here," said Max. "Check this out."

Henry followed Max to a locker on the far side of the room. Above the locker was his name, Henry Fredrickson, in large bold letters. Inside the locker hung a white Breakers uniform and a brand-new tennis racquet.

"What do you think?" asked Max.

"Is that stuff mine?" asked Henry.

"You bet it is," said Max. "They're gifts from my dad. Get dressed, and we'll head to the courts."

The indoor courts were in another part of the building. Henry couldn't believe his eyes when they walked in. There were sixteen courts in two rows of eight. The first eight courts each had ball machines, like the ones Henry had seen on TV. Those courts were for practicing hitting.

"Let's practice next to each other," said Max. He handed Henry a tiny remote control. "Here's the controller. Push the green button when you're ready."

Max jogged to a court. Henry ran to the next court.

Suddenly Max's ball machine came to life and started firing balls across the net. Max hit a couple of nice shots back.

Henry pressed the green button on his controller. An instant later, a ball shot toward him. Henry lined up the ball and smacked a shot over the net.

"Nice!" yelled Max.

The balls kept coming as the machine moved back and forth. It fired shots to both Henry's forehand and backhand sides. "This is awesome!" shouted Henry.

"I know!" yelled Max. "Welcome to the team!"

Other players came in, each player entering a court. Soon, eight players were warming up against the ball machines.

Then Max's dad walked in. Mr. Martinson let them practice for a while longer. Then he led the team through a dozen different drills. Finally, it was time to play a match. Henry and Max played against each other.

On the last point of the match, Henry hit a ball deep into Max's court. Max fired back a shot to Henry's forehand. Henry set up for the shot. He waited for just the right moment. Then he blasted the ball into the court and past Max.

"Yes!" Henry yelled.

Henry and Max met at the net. "Nice shot," said Max shaking Henry's hand.

"Nice match," said Henry, smiling.

"Now, are you ready to go to the pool?" asked Max.

"There's a pool?" asked Henry.

"Of course there is," said Max. "There's an outdoor pool with cold drinks, lounge chairs, and cute girls. And we can order whatever we want for lunch and bill it to my dad. Let's go!"

Max took off running. Henry chased him, yelling, "This is even better than you said it would be!"

CHAPTER 5

THE FIRST MATCH

Henry bounced a tennis ball on the court. He looked across the net at his opponent. It was the sixth game of the first real match of the indoor season. The Breakers were playing against the Penn Tennis Club Aces.

Henry was ahead four games to one in the first set. Just two more games and he would win the set. Then, if he won another set, he would win the match.

He bounced the ball once more. Then he threw it high into the air. He slammed the ball with his racquet. The ball soared over the net.

His opponent slid to his right and hit a hard shot back. Henry moved forward a little. He hit the ball deep across the net. The other player hit it back.

Henry then sent a shot to the other corner. His opponent tried to get to it, but couldn't. Henry won the point.

On the next point, Henry hit a serve so hard that his opponent didn't even touch it. Ace!

Henry was on a roll. Next, he went to the net and smashed a hard, fast shot right at his opponent's feet. Then the score was 40–0.

Henry lined up his next serve. He bounced the ball four times, then threw the ball up into the air. He pounded the ball with his racquet and raced to the net.

The other player hit a lob over Henry's head instead of trying to hit a shot past him. Henry had no choice but to race back to get the ball after it bounced.

Henry ran back to the end of the court. He got there just in time to hit a shot back across the net. It was a short shot, though, so his opponent came to the net and hit a bullet back toward Henry.

This time, Henry was ready for it. He took one step back, pulled his racquet behind his right side and hit a killer shot past the reaching arm of his opponent. The game was over.

Henry was ahead 5–1 in the set. One more game and he'd win.

The players got ready for the next game. Henry bounced back and forth on his toes as his opponent prepared to serve.

Henry won that game without breaking a sweat. He had won the first set easily, six games to one.

As the two players took a break between sets, Henry sat on the bench. He smiled happily. He was playing the game he loved in a totally awesome indoor tennis club, and he was winning his first match of the season.

After a quick drink of water, he jumped to his feet and raced onto the court, ready to start the next set.

CHAPTER 6

THE LEAGUE FEE LIE

Henry was on a winning streak. He'd won the match against his opponent from the Aces. Two days later, he beat a player from the Prestwood Strings.

Hours after winning his third match in a row the following Saturday, Henry sat in his living room. There was a professional tennis tournament on TV.

"Hi, Henry," said his dad, entering the room.

"Hey, Dad," said Henry, keeping his eyes on the TV.

"What is this?" his dad asked.

Henry turned around. His dad held up his new tennis bag. Usually, Henry tucked it under his bed when he got home from the tennis club.

I forgot to hide it, he thought nervously.

"It's my tennis bag," said Henry. He sat up straighter in his chair.

"I can see that," said his dad. "It's new. And the racquet is new too. Do you want to tell me where they came from?"

"Max's dad, Coach Martinson, gave them to me," said Henry.

"Why did he give you these things?" his father asked. "And why didn't you tell us?"

"He's the coach," Henry explained. "He was just being nice. I guess I didn't tell you because I was afraid you wouldn't let me keep them."

"Henry, I'm not happy about this," said his dad. "We don't keep secrets in this family. You know that."

"I know, Dad," said Henry. "I'm sorry."

"I want you to ask Mr. Martinson how much he paid for these things," Henry's dad said. "Then I want to pay him back. You got that?"

"But Dad, they were gifts," said Henry.

"Don't argue with me," Dad said, shaking his head. "You find out how much they cost, and then I'll pay him back."

"Okay," Henry said quietly.

"Are there any other secrets about this tennis league you've been keeping from us?" Dad asked.

Henry looked down at the carpet.

"Henry," said his dad. "I asked you a question."

"No, Dad," said Henry. "No other secrets."

Henry felt terrible for lying. But he knew that if he told his dad that Max's dad had paid his league fees, Dad would make him quit the team.

"Good," said his dad. "When you're done watching that match, go outside and mow the lawn, okay?"

"Sure," said Henry. His dad left the room. Henry sunk down into his chair.

He felt awful. His dad had asked him about the league, and Henry had lied right to his face. He hadn't lied to his dad since he stole a candy bar from the gas station when he was five.

Henry didn't feel like watching TV anymore. He turned it off and headed to the back yard.

CHAPTER 7

A STEP BACKWARD

Henry's winning streak ended after the conversation with his dad. He lost the next two matches he played.

A week later, Henry was playing against a member of the Inglewood Smashers. The Breakers were hosting a tournament with three other teams.

Henry was down in the match, one set to nothing. He was losing the second set, five games to two.

"Come on, Henry!" Max shouted from the bleachers. "You can definitely beat this guy!"

Henry bounced on his feet and waited for his opponent to serve. He watched a strong serve come to his left side. Henry took a step in that direction and hit a backhand.

The ball sailed over the baseline on the other side of the net. It was a point for his opponent. 15–0.

Henry moved back into place and waited for the next serve. He was starting to see his opponent's strategy. The other player must have noticed that Henry's backhand side was weak, because he was hitting everything to Henry's left.

Great, Henry thought.

He'd lost all of his confidence in his backhand. During the last week, his backhand had gone from bad to worse. He could hardly hit anything that went to his left side.

Once again, Henry watched as his opponent served to his left. Henry managed to hit a weak shot over the net. His opponent pounced on the ball, drilling a winning shot into the corner. 30–0.

"You can do it, Henry," yelled Max. "It's not over until it's over!"

The next serve came to his left too. Henry reached back and hit the ball with the edge of his racquet, sending it into the net. 40–0.

It was match point. If Henry lost one more point, he'd lose.

Henry got into position. The serve sailed over the net, and Henry reached for it. He put everything he had into his shot. His swing was smooth. He hit the ball well, but his opponent had raced to the net after the serve, so he was in perfect position.

His opponent waited for Henry's shot. Then he smashed the ball into the court and away from Henry for the win. The match was over.

Henry shook hands with his opponent. Then he went to the end of the court, where Max was waiting for him.

"Tough match," said Max. "It's that backhand. Don't worry. It will get better."

"My backhand isn't the problem," said Henry. "Well, it's part of the problem, but it's not the main part. It's my dad."

"Your dad?" asked Max. "What about him?"

Henry sighed. "I feel bad about lying to him," he said. "You've seen how I've been playing tennis lately. I stink. And it's because of the lie."

"So what are you going to do?" asked Max.

"I'm going to tell him," said Henry. "Even if it means I have to quit the team. I'd rather be honest with my dad than play tennis. I'm going to tell him tonight, right after the tournament."

"You might not have to wait that long," said Max. "Look." He pointed toward the arena doors.

Henry turned to look. His mom and dad were walking into the arena.

CHAPTER 8

THE SECRET'S OUT

Henry felt a lump form in his throat as he watched his parents walk in.

"What are you going to do?" asked Max.

"I'm going to go tell them," said Henry.

"Now?" asked Max. "Can't you wait until after the tournament? What if your dad makes you quit the team?"

"I've already waited long enough," said Henry.

He jogged over to the bleachers, where his parents were standing. "Hey, guys," he said. "I'm glad you could make it."

"Of course, bud," said Henry's dad. "Sorry we couldn't get here earlier."

"How did you do in your first match?" asked Henry's mom.

"I lost pretty bad," said Henry.

"That's too bad," said his dad. "I'm sure you played great, though."

"I guess," Henry said. He looked down at his shoes. He was struggling to find the courage to say what he needed to say.

"Hey, Henry, are these your parents?" someone asked.

Henry looked up. It was Coach Martinson.

"We sure are," Henry's dad said proudly. He reached out to shake Coach Martinson's hand.

"It's just great to finally meet you both," said Coach. "I can't tell you how happy I am that Henry is playing with us in the indoor league. He's a super player and a great kid."

"Thanks," said Henry's mom. "We're really happy that you're coaching him and letting him play on the team."

"I wouldn't have it any other way," said Coach Martinson. "And I know the fees are pretty expensive, so I'm really glad you let me pay for Henry. It was my pleasure, since he's so talented."

Dad frowned. "What do you mean?" he asked.

"Henry's league fees," said Coach. "I know that most people just don't have that kind of money lying around. I was happy to pay for Henry."

The proud smile disappeared from Henry's dad's face. "Yeah, thanks," he said. "Well, it was nice to meet you, Coach Martinson."

"Nice to meet you too," said Coach.

As the coach walked away, Henry felt sick to his stomach. He looked down at his feet.

For a few seconds, no one spoke. Then Dad asked, "What was Coach Martinson talking about?"

Henry didn't look up. Mom sighed and said, "I think you owe us both an explanation, Henry."

"I was going to tell you," said Henry. Suddenly, the words just poured out. "I was just about to tell you. Right before Coach Martinson walked up. Honest. I was going to tell you that I had lied to you about the league fees."

He took a deep breath. Then he went on, "I was going to apologize and tell you that I would be willing to quit the team if you wanted me to. I'm so sorry, Mom. I'm sorry, Dad. I didn't mean to lie to you. Really. I didn't mean to."

Henry wiped a tear from his cheek. He looked down at the ground again.

Dad shook his head. "You've been lying to us this whole time, and now you expect us to believe that you were just about to tell us the truth?" he said. "Why should we believe you now?"

"Because it is the truth, Dad," said Henry. "Please believe me."

A message rang out from the loudspeaker. "The singles match between Hans Humphrey and Henry Fredrickson will begin in five minutes. Players, please report to court two immediately," the voice said.

"You better go," Dad said.

"Wait, Dad," said Henry. "Can't we talk about this?"

"We will later," said his dad. Then he turned and walked out the arena doors.

"Just go," Mom said. "Go play your match. Your dad and I will talk to you at home."

Henry sighed. Then he slowly walked out to the courts.

CHAPTER 9

ANOTHER TOUGH MATCH

Twenty minutes into the next match, Henry was on his way to another loss. The score in the first set was five games to nothing.

During the match, Henry had been keeping a constant eye on the bleachers. The entire time, his mom had been sitting there by herself.

But now, as Henry looked through the crowd, he couldn't find her.

Henry waited for his opponent's serve. *Why did Mom leave?* he wondered nervously.

The serve flew toward him. He reacted quickly and hit the ball hard across the net. His opponent hit a shot to Henry's backhand. Henry tried to get a good shot on the ball, but all he could manage was to hit a lazy floater back.

His opponent wound up and smashed a rocket to Henry's forehand. Henry lunged, but missed the ball. The score was 15–0.

The next serve went to Henry's backhand. He hit the ball into the net. 30–0. Then the following serve bounced high to his right. Henry nailed the shot way too hard, sending the ball far past the baseline.

Another point to his opponent. 40–0.

Henry shook his head angrily. *I can't do anything right*, he thought.

As his opponent got ready to serve, Henry looked out at the bleachers again. His mom was back, and Henry's dad was sitting next to her.

Henry smiled nervously at his parents. His dad looked at him, but he didn't smile back.

Henry's concentration was gone. He lost the game and the set. *That's it*, he thought. *There's no way I'll win the match.*

Before the next set, he took a break on the bench. As he drank from his water bottle, he heard his mom's voice. "Your dad came back," she said.

Henry turned around. "I know," he said quietly.

"That's a big deal for him," Mom said. "He is very upset. I am too. You've never lied to us before, and it really hurt us."

"I know, Mom," said Henry.

"It's going to take a lot to make this up to us," said his mom. "But right now, we want you to know that we support you. We love you, and we know we can work this out."

"Thanks, Mom," said Henry. He smiled, and his mother smiled back.

"Now get out there and show everybody what you've got," said his mom.

CHAPTER 10

BACK IN THE GAME

The bounce in Henry's game returned in the second set. He was glad. It made a big difference to know that his parents were behind him.

He was relieved that they seemed willing to help him work through his mistake. Now, Henry could put his concentration on tennis again.

Everything was going well. Even his backhand seemed to have improved.

Henry raced around the court, getting to shots he would have been unable to get to earlier in the match.

Henry was quickly winning points and dominating the match. He wanted to win, but he also wanted to show his dad why he loved tennis so much. He wanted to play his best match ever.

He won the second set. Soon, Henry was up four games to three in the third set. If he won two more games he would win the match.

As he waited for his opponent to serve, Henry leaned forward, swaying back and forth. He held his racquet in both hands.

The serve came blasting across the net. Henry moved to his left and hit a sharp backhand return.

His opponent ran to the ball and hit a strong shot deep into Henry's court. Henry stepped back and hit a forehand into the far right corner. His opponent hit a slow shot back.

Henry waited for the ball to bounce high to his forehand side. Then he ripped a winner past his opponent's racquet. He was winning.

The next two points went his way too. Henry used more hard shots to keep his opponent on his heels. Then his opponent fired two solid serves to win the next two points.

With the score at 30–40, the players hit shot after shot to each other for several minutes. Finally, Henry won the point when his opponent hit a shot into the net.

Henry felt great — confident and strong. He had found his game again, and his parents were there to see it happen.

The score in the set was five games to three. Henry was serving to win the match. He bounced the ball a couple more times, and then went into his serve.

The ball flew across the net. His opponent didn't even move. Ace! 15–0.

Henry lined up the next serve, and fired another ace, then another. He was ahead 40–0. Henry smiled. Then he positioned himself behind the baseline for match point.

Slowly, Henry bounced the ball, then served to his opponent. The other player got to the ball and hit a deep shot back to Henry.

It came to Henry's left, his backhand. *Stay calm*, Henry thought.

He set himself up for the shot. Then he took one last look at his opponent, waiting at the net.

Finally, when the ball arrived, Henry ripped a backhand with everything he had. The shot sailed past the diving racquet of his opponent and into the court for a winner.

The game was over. Henry had won the match.

"Great game!" Max yelled from the stands. Henry smiled at him.

Henry shook hands with his opponent, but all he could think about was talking to his parents. He rushed over to meet them at the end of the court.

Henry looked at his dad. "I'm so sorry I lied to you," Henry said quietly.

"I know you are, kiddo," Dad said.

"You guys have every right to be mad at me," Henry said.

"We're not mad," Mom said.

"You're not?" Henry asked hopefully.

"No, we're not," Dad said. "We're just disappointed."

"So I guess you want me to quit the team," Henry said.

His mom frowned and asked, "Quit? What do you mean?"

"How could we let you quit?" Dad added. "After seeing you play? No way. We're not going to let you quit. You're way too good."

"But what about the fees?" asked Henry. "What about the lie?"

"We'll get through this together," said his dad. "We'll figure it out as a family."

"No more secrets, right?" Mom asked.

"No more secrets," said Henry. "I'll make this up to both of you. And I'll do anything to keep playing tennis."

ABOUT THE AUTHOR

Chris Kreie lives in Minnesota with his wife and two children. He works as a school librarian, and in his free time he writes books like this. Some of his other books in this series include *Wild Hike* and *Gridiron Bully*.

ABOUT THE ILLUSTRATOR

When Sean Tiffany was growing up, he lived on a small island off the coast of Maine. Every day, from sixth grade until he graduated from high school, he had to take a boat to get to school. When Sean isn't working on his art, he works on a multimedia project called "OilCan Drive," which combines music and art. He has a pet cactus named Jim.

GLOSSARY

apologize (uh-POL-uh-jize)—say that you are sorry about something

cocked (KOKD)—turned up to one side

concentration (kon-suhn-TRAY-shuhn)—all of your thoughts and attention

conversation (kon-vur-SAY-shuhn)—a talk

convinced (kuhn-VINSSD)—made someone believe something

dominating (DOM-uh-nate-ing)—controlling or ruling

explanation (ek-spluh-NAY-shuhn)—a reason for something

receptionist (ri-SEP-shuh-nist)—a person whose job is to greet people

strategy (STRAT-uh-jee)—a clever plan for winning

unbelievable (uhn-bi-LEEV-uh-buhl)—so strange, amazing, or surprising that it is hard to believe it is true

TENNIS WORDS YOU SHOULD KNOW

ace (AYSS)—a serve that is not returned, or even touched, by the other player

backhand (BAK-hand)—a stroke that you play with your arm across your body and the back of your hand facing outward

baseline (BAYSS-line)—the line marking each end of the court

floater (FLOHT-ur)—a slow shot, which gives the other player time to set up a return shot

forehand (FOR-hand)—a stroke that you play wtih the palm of your hand facing outward

game (GAYM)—in tennis, a game is over when one player reaches 45 points

league (LEEG)—a group of sports teams

lob (LAHB)—to throw or hit a ball high into the air

match (MACH)—in tennis, a match is won when a player wins two sets

match point (MACH POINT)—the final point in the match

opponent (uh-POH-nuhnt)—someone who is against you in a fight, contest, or game

racquet (RAK-it)—a stringed frame with a handle that you use in games like tennis, badminton, and squash

serve (SURV)—to begin play by hitting the ball

set (SET)—in tennis, a set is won when a player wins six games, and has won at least two more games than his or her opponent

singles (SING-guhlz)—a match played by one player against another. Doubles is a match played by two players against two others.

trophy (TROH-fee)—a prize given to a winning athlete

DISCUSSION QUESTIONS

1. Why did Henry lie to his parents?

2. Max's dad pays Henry's fees and buys him new tennis equipment. What are some other ways that Henry could have gotten the money?

3. In this book, Max and Henry play tennis during the summer. What do you like to do during the summer? What do other kids at your school do? Talk about different ways to have fun during the summer.

WRITING PROMPTS

1. Henry lied to his mom and dad. Write about a time that you lied to your parents. What happened? How did you resolve the problem?

2. Henry's dad wants him to play football, but Henry wants to play tennis. Write about something that your parents wanted you to do. Did you do it? Why or why not?

3. At the end of this book, Henry says he'll do anything to make up for lying to his parents. What do you think he does? Write about it.

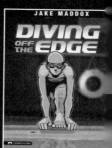

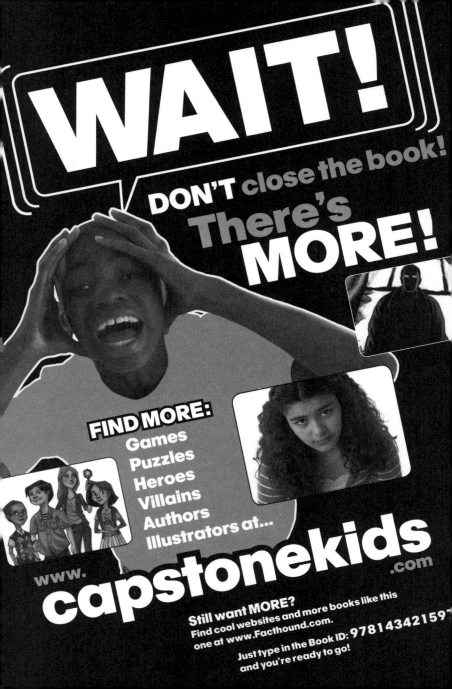